Split! Splat!

BY **AMY GIBSON**

ILLUSTRATED BY **STEVE BJÖRKMAN**

SCHOLASTIC INC.
New York Toronto London Auckland
Sydney Mexico City New Delhi Hong Kong

ISBN 978-0-545-46409-3

12 11 10 9 8 7 6 5 4 3   13 14 15 16 17/0

Printed in the U.S.A.   40

First Scholastic paperback printing, April 2012

The text was set in MrsEaves. The display type was set in P22Garamouche.

Book design by Marijka Kostiw

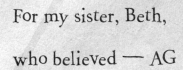

For my sister, Beth,

who believed — AG

For my adventurous daughter,

Kristi, who finds joy in exploring

all kinds of weather — SB

I sing a little rain song,

a simple song,

a plain song,

a pitter-patter-tip-tap-
on-the-windowpane song.

Pip

pip

pip

pip,

drippy drop drop drip.

Tip
tap,
pit
pat,
pitter patter split splat!

Splishy sploshy wishy washy —

drip

drip

drop!

I sing a little mud song,
a puddle song,
a muddle song,

a no-shoes, toes-ooze,
slip-slap-and-thud song.

Splish
sploosh,
squash
squoosh,

oochy sploochy woochy woosh!

Slip

slop,

ker-plop!

Mucka mucka chucka wucka —

splish

splash

sploosh!

I sing a little sun song,
a fun song,
a run song,

a clouds-gone,
green-lawn,
raining-is-all-done song.

Swish
swish
swish
swish,

swishy swash wish wash.

Tickle wiggle wriggle giggle,

hop

skip,

back flip —

jump thump rump

BUMP —

skip

flip

flop!

I sing a little rain song,
a mud song,
a sun song,

a clouds-cry,
mud-pie,
bluc sky
song.